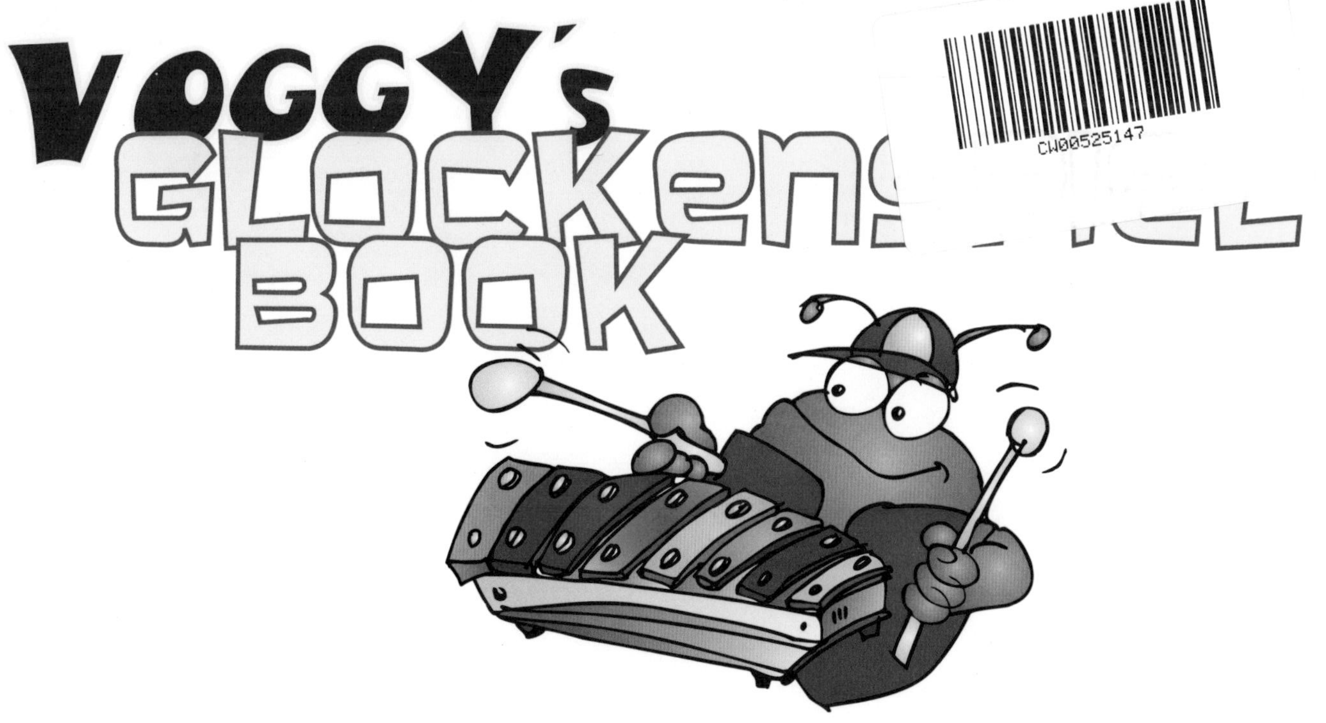


*This book belongs to:*

..........................................................

*Conception and manuscript: Martina Holtz*
*Composition (P. 25, 27, 29, 32, 34, 54, 64, 68, 70): Martina Holtz*
*Lyrics (38, 42, 50, 58): Martina Holtz*

*Cover design and illustrations: OZ, Essen (Katrin & Christian Brackmann)*


*Viktoriastr. 25, D-53173 Bonn/Germany*
*www.voggenreiter.de*
*info@voggenreiter.de*

*ISBN: 3-8024-0460-2*

03

# Hello!

*Hello. My name is Voggy, and it will be my pleasure to accompany you through this glockenspiel tutorial!*
*My simple explanations and lots of funny drawings will show you how to have heaps of fun with your glockenspiel. It's a good idea to ask your parents to go through this book with you because they will be able to help you find the answers to the little quizzes that I have hidden on these pages. With many of the tunes that you will find in this book you will see me holding a CD in my hand, which means that you can play along to this tune found on the accompanying music CD. You'll find a more thorough explanation on page 78.*

*So, off you go! I hope you have lots of fun with this book and a wonderful time with your glockenspiel.*

*Voggy*

# Contents

# Your Glockenspiel

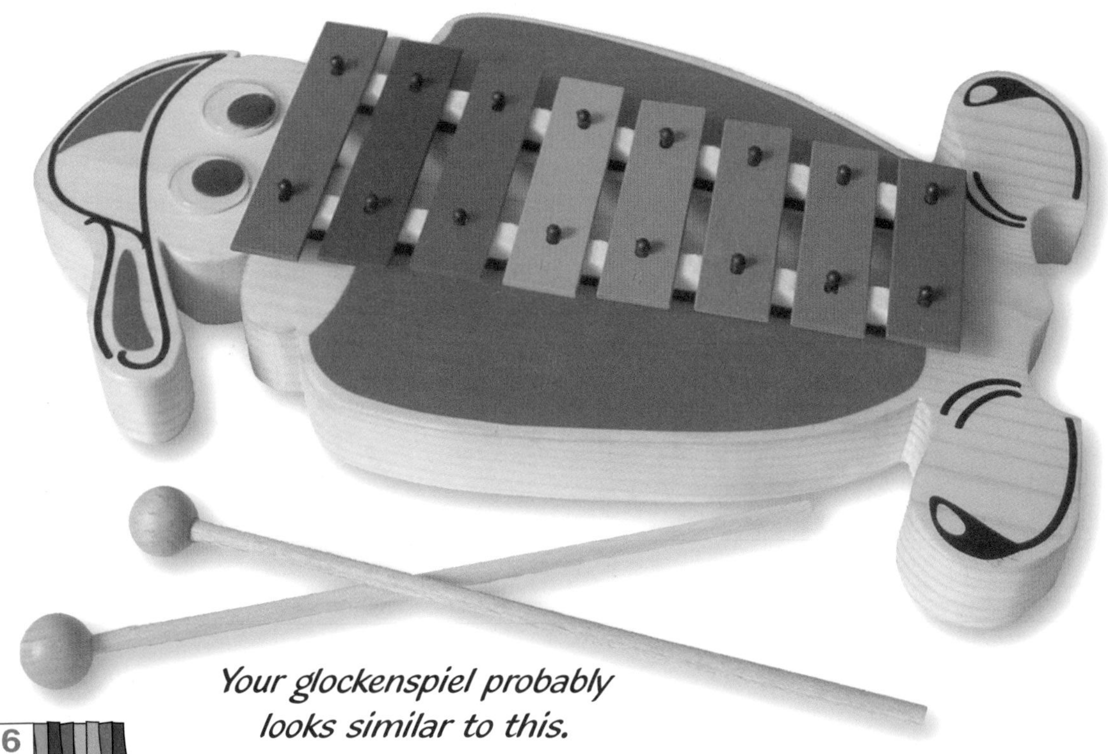

*Your glockenspiel probably looks similar to this.*

*This is how the bars are attached to your glockenspiel. The bars should rest lightly on top of the felt underlay.*

*If the small pins holding the bars are bent and the bars are trapped, the tones produced will not sound as clear as they should.*

# How to produce the best sound

*There are many ways to play a glockenspiel.
Here are some of them!*

*You can play it 'normally' with the heads of your mallets.*

*Try hitting the bars with the other end of your mallets.*

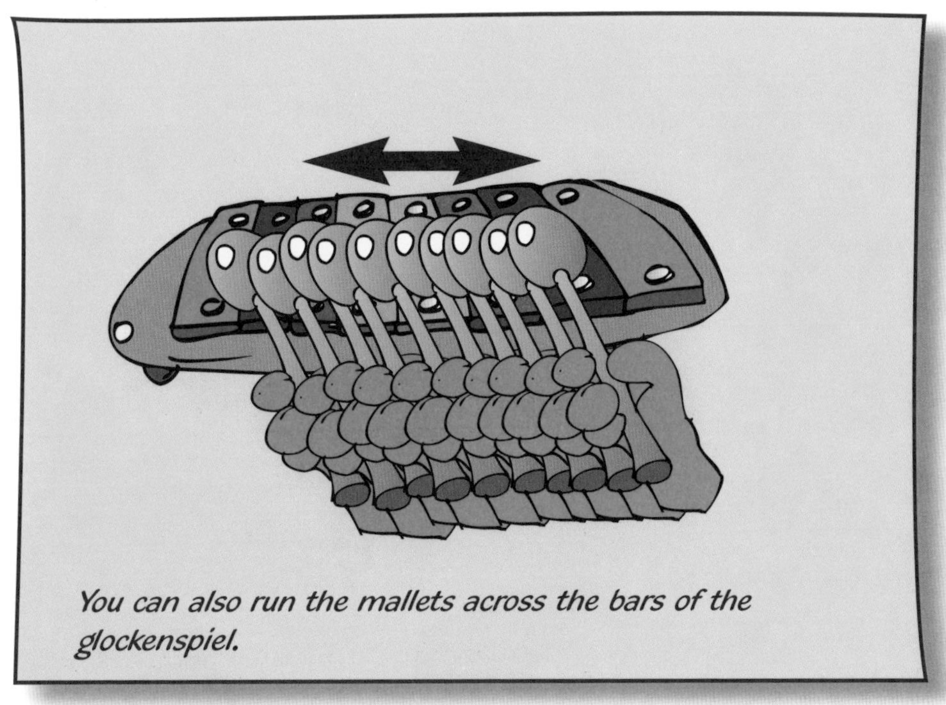

*You can also run the mallets across the bars of the glockenspiel.*

*You're sure to think of lots of other ways of playing ... experiment a little and listen to the sound you produce.*

# Hopping?

*You probably noticed that the best sound is produced when you hit the bars of your glockenspiel with the heads of your mallets. Now just imagine that the head of one of the mallets is little Voggy, jumping around on the glocken-spiel, first on one bar and then back and forth between two bars.*

*When you have managed that, try hopping on all the bars, one after the other. It's best to start with the largest bar.*
*Simply imagine them as planks of wood lying on the surface of a lake. But take care not to fall between them, otherwise ...*

# *Counting!*

*So that it's easier to make music later,*
*we'll try out a little exercise first.*
*Count nice and evenly from **one to four**.*
*Then repeat the exercise. That's all.*

*And now we'll repeat the counting exercise again and clap at the same time (on every number).*

*If you prefer, you can count and hit a bar of the glocken-spiel with one of your mallets instead of clapping.*

# Quarter Notes (Crotchets)

*Notes tell you how to play tones and a note exists for every tone that you can play. (Did you notice that notes look almost the same as your mallets?!)*

*Quarter notes have a black note head and a note stem.*

***Note stem***

***Note head***

***Quarter notes*** *look like this.*

*For every quarter note you have to strike your glockenspiel once, which is why we sometimes call them one-beat notes. Here you see eight notes, which means you play eight tones. Choose a bar on your glockenspiel and hit it once for every note. Count along at the same time to the numbers found above the notes.*

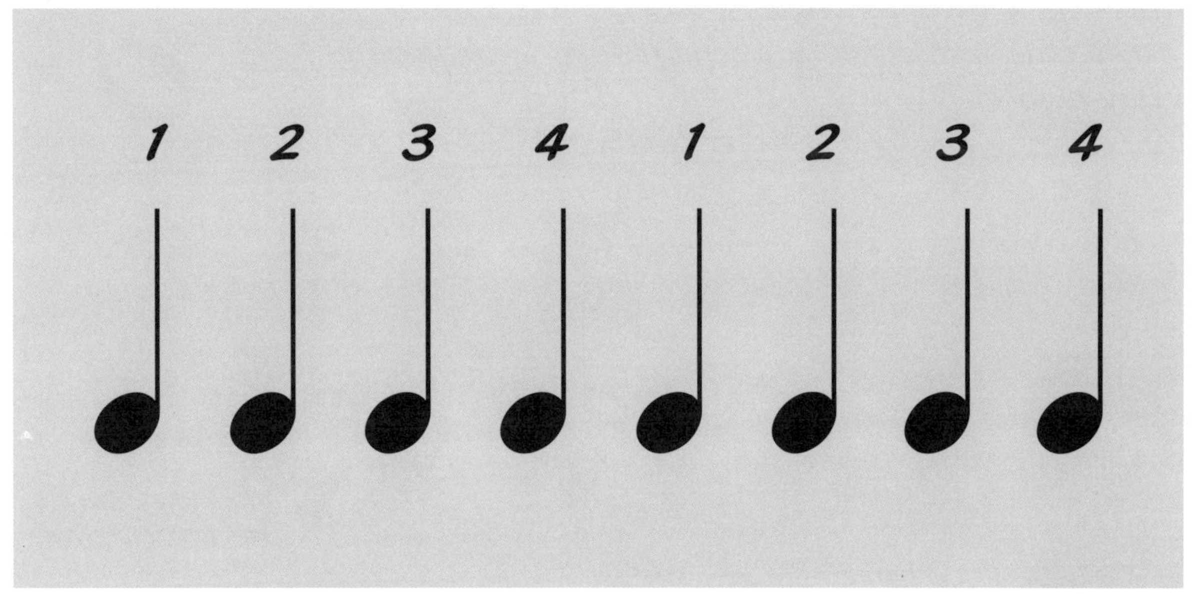

# Half Notes (Minims)

*This note is called a **half note.** It looks almost the same as the quarter note but it has a white, unfilled note head. This note is twice as long as a quarter note. So you play a tone/note on every second number instead of on every number.*
*You can hear the tone last over two beats.*

***Half note***

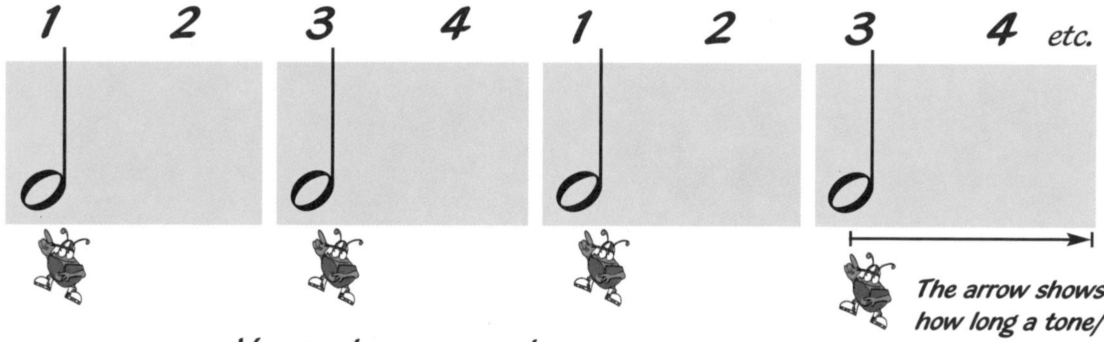


***The arrow shows you how long a tone/note lasts.***

*Voggy shows you when to play a note.*

*Try playing these notes on the largest bar. Listen to them on the CD first. Voggy is showing you which number to listen to on the CD.*

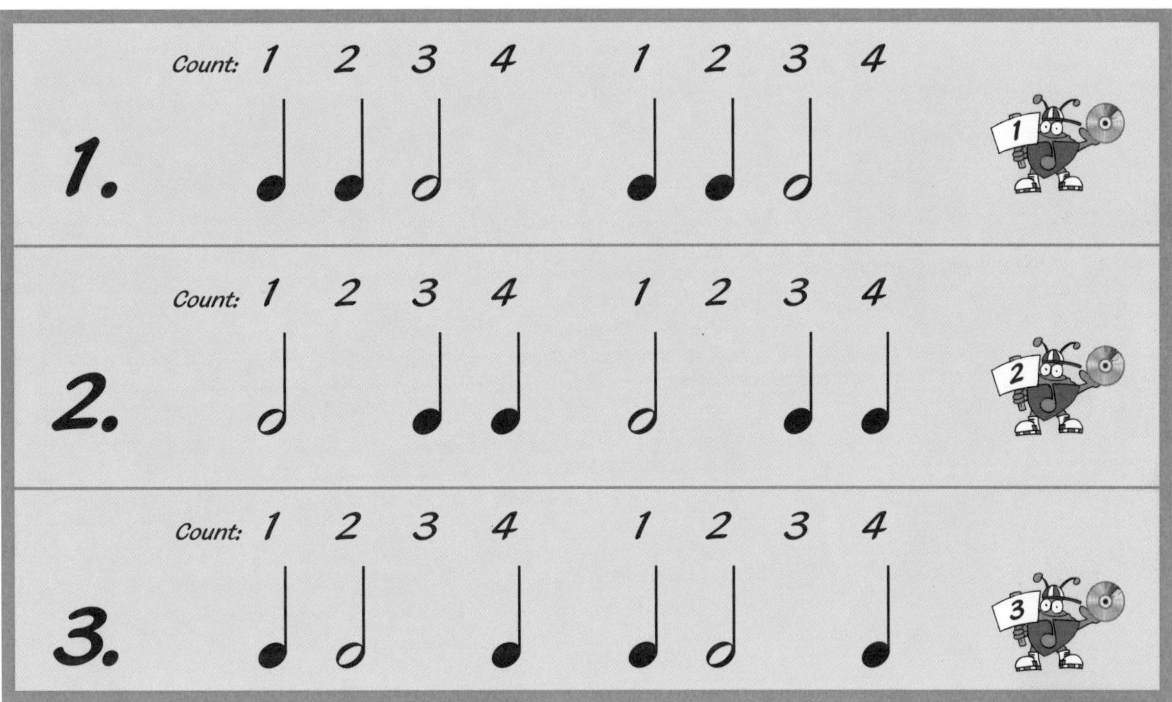

# *Lines of the Staff*

*We have already become familiar with rhythm – now all we need to know is which note to play or, in other words, which bar to hit on the glockenspiel.*

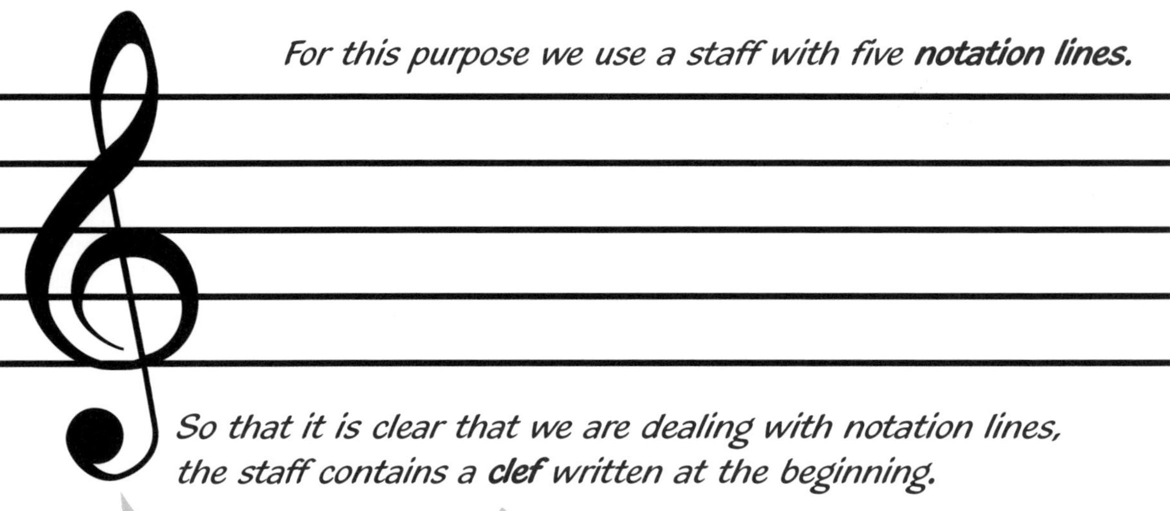

*For this purpose we use a staff with five **notation lines.***

*So that it is clear that we are dealing with notation lines, the staff contains a **clef** written at the beginning.*

*The note heads are either written on the lines or in the spaces between them.*

# C, Your First Note

The first note, C, is so low that it no longer fits on the staff. We therefore need a short ledger line to notate this note below the staff. So that you can recognize it more easily, we will color the head of the note C green.

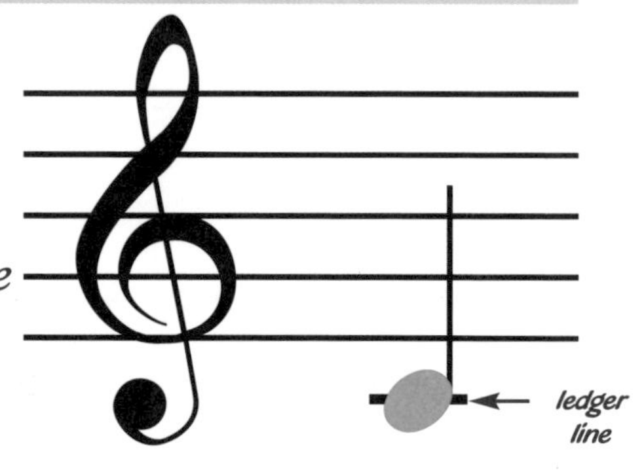


The Note C

C is the lowest note on your glockenspiel. Strike the largest bar on the far left of your glockenspiel. The bar on Voggy's glockenspiel is also colored green.


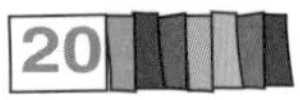

# Color this picture!

# Bar Lines

*To make it easier to count notes, we have counted from **one to four** each time. In order to be able to see these groups of four easily on the sheet of music, the groups have lines between them.*
*We call these lines **bar lines**.*

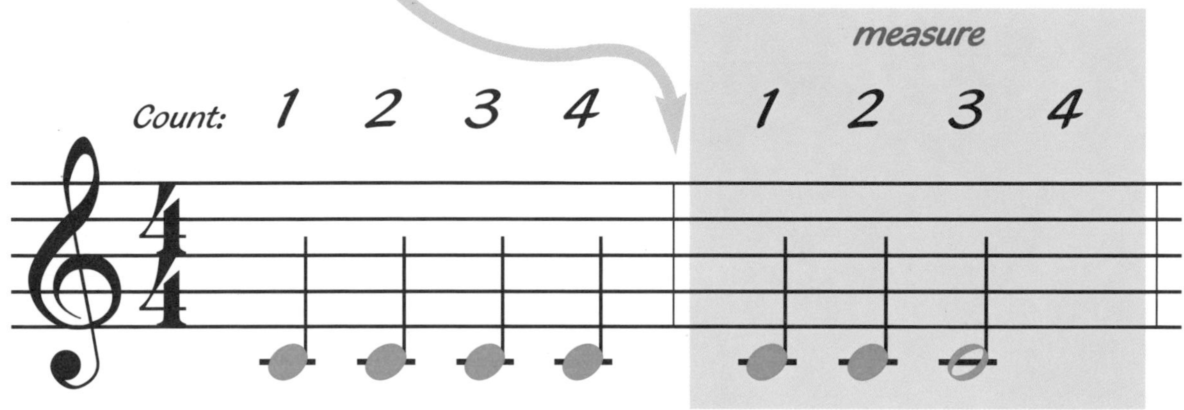


*A **measure** is what we call the contents between two bar lines.*

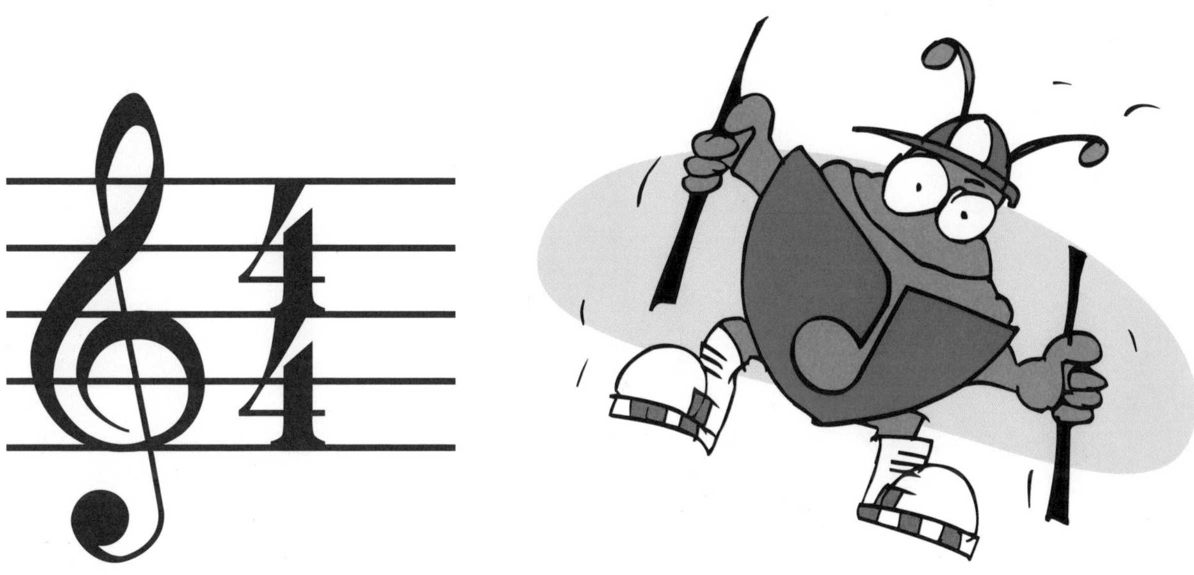

*So that you know that you always need to count to four, the symbol **4/4** is written after the clef.*

# Measure or Cake?

*You can imagine a measure as a cake cut into several pieces. It doesn't matter how big each piece of cake is, together they still represent one cake.*

*Measures are dealt with in exactly the same way. There should be no missing notes – you must always be able to count to four.*

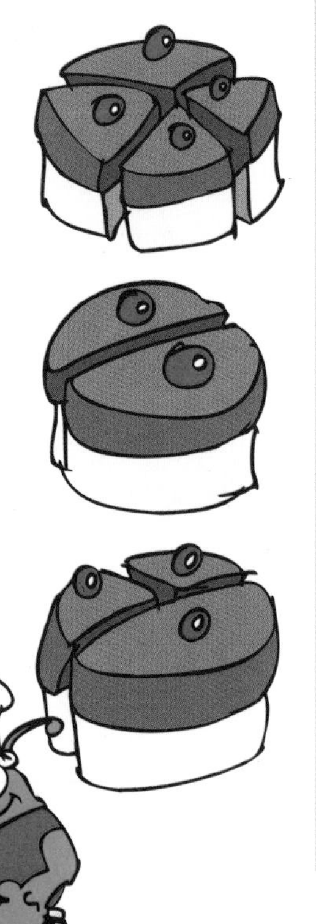

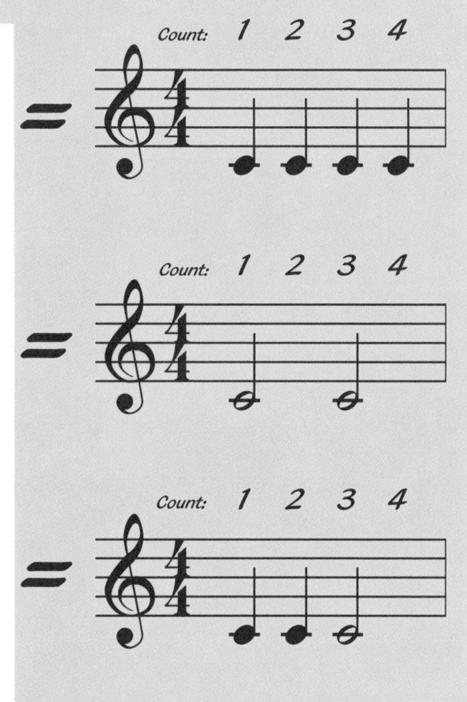

*Try playing the tune below. When you have finished playing the first staff, carry on at the beginning of the next one.*

# Skate on Ice

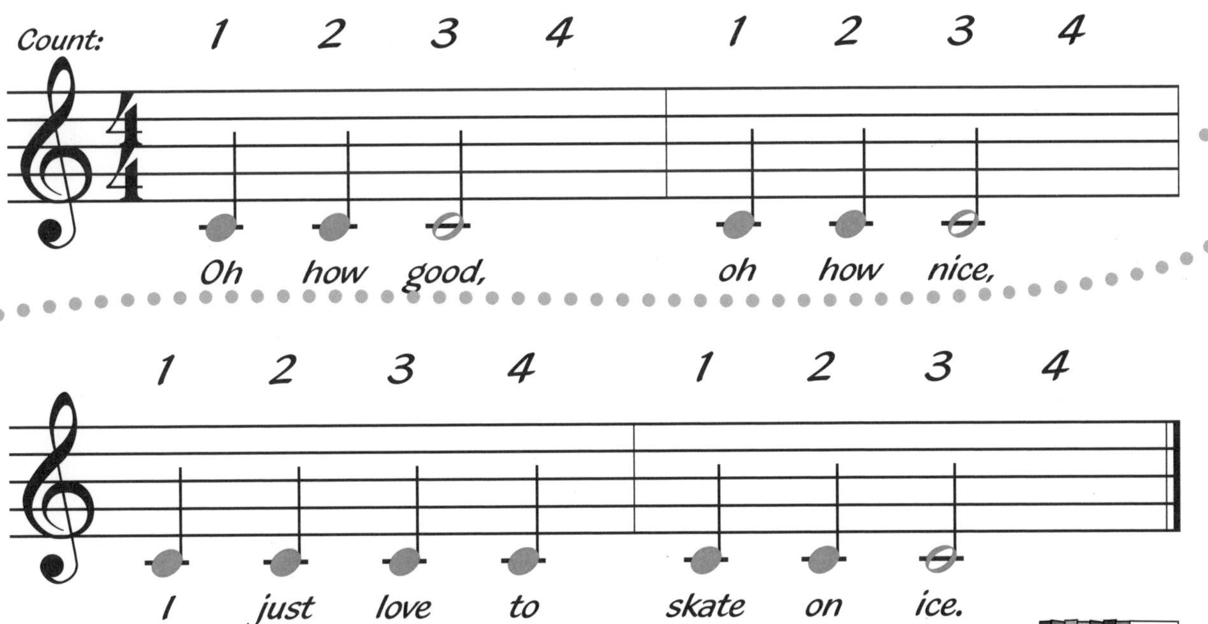

# The Second Note: D

The note D

The note D lies directly above C. Its note head lies directly below the bottom line of the staff. We have colored this note **brown.**

Simply play the second largest bar on your glockenspiel. It is located to the right of C.

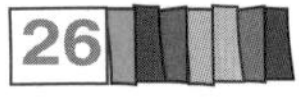

# The Mouse

*With the two notes C and D you can already play your second tune.*

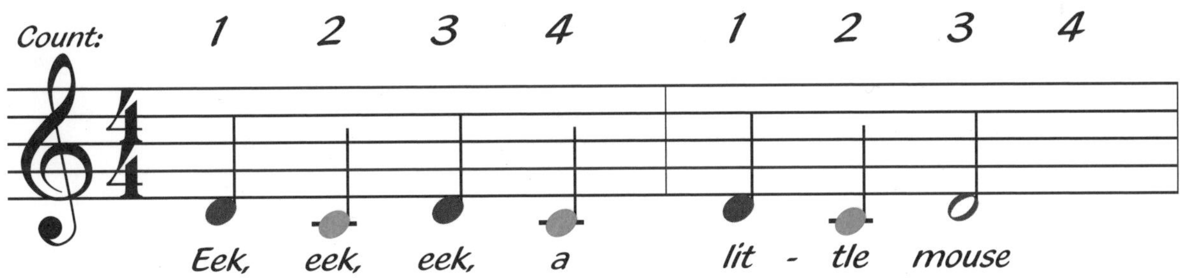


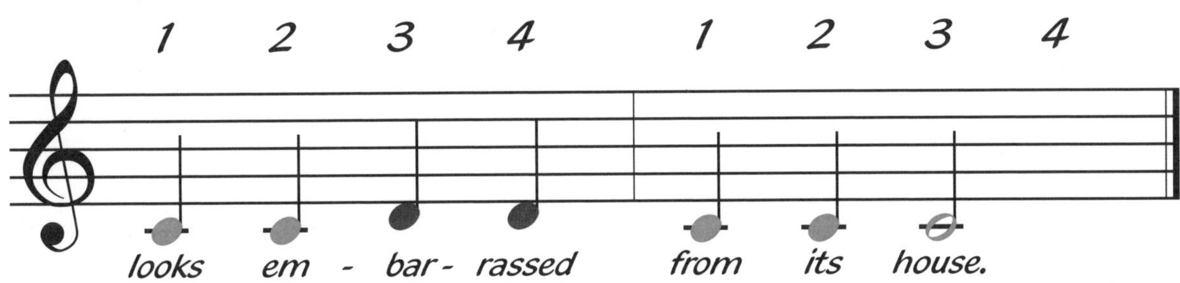

# The Third Note: E

*The third bar on your glockenspiel is the note E. We'll use the color red. This note can be found directly on the bottom line of the staff.*

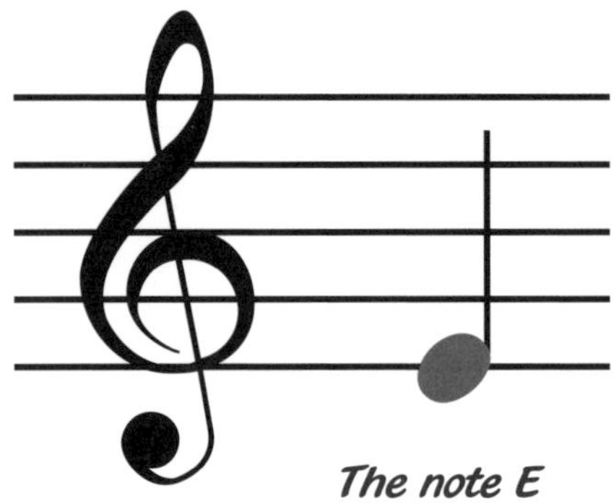

***The note E***

# Dancing 'Round

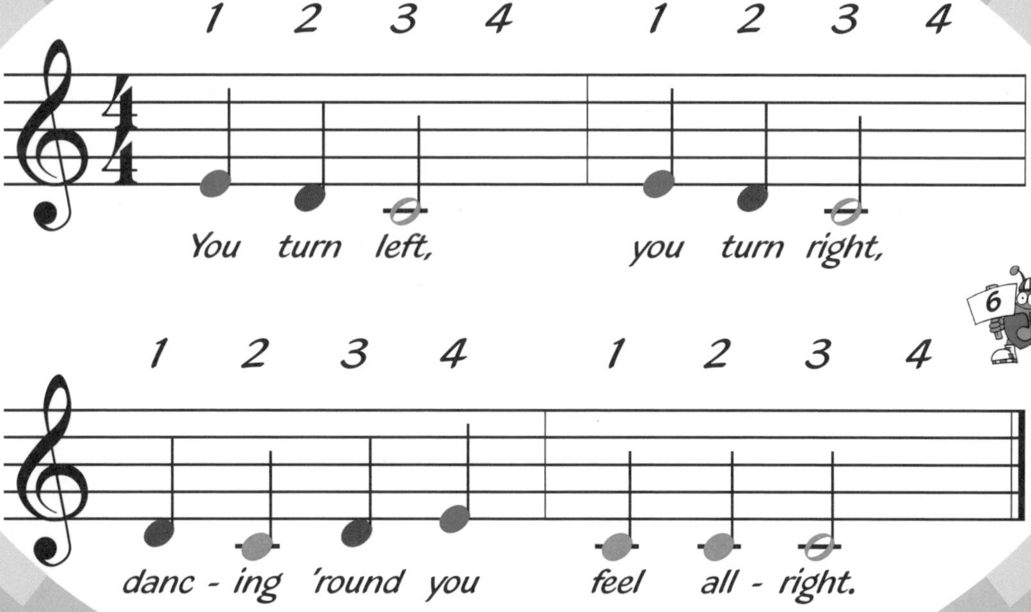

1 2 3 4 1 2 3 4

You turn left, you turn right,

6

1 2 3 4 1 2 3 4

danc - ing 'round you feel all - right.

# F Comes After E

*One note higher up the scale than E lies F.*
*We will color this note yellow.*
*F lies in the space between the first two notation lines from the bottom of the staff.*

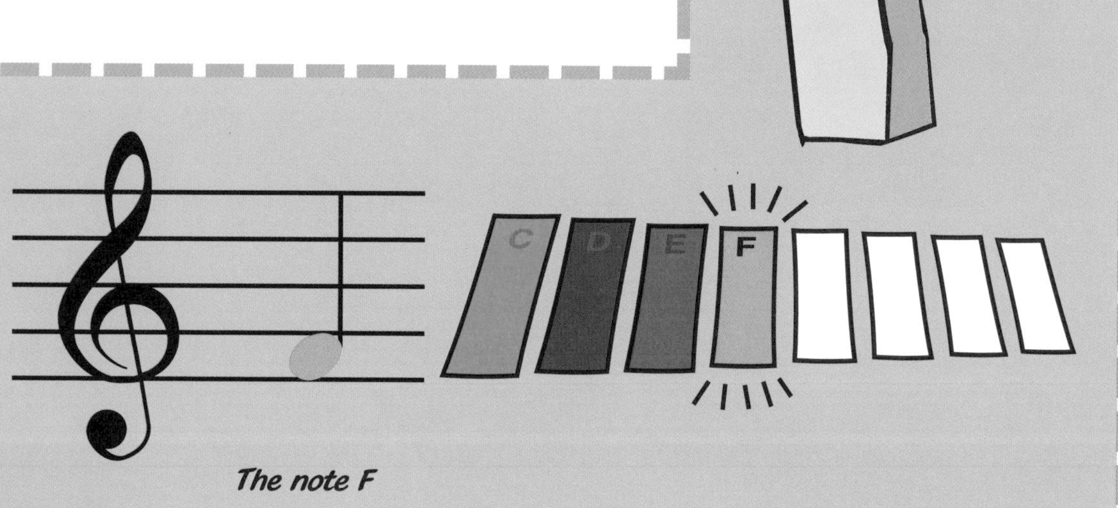


*The note F*

# Do You Remember All the Notes?

*Write the names of the notes in the boxes.*
*See p. 74 for answers.*

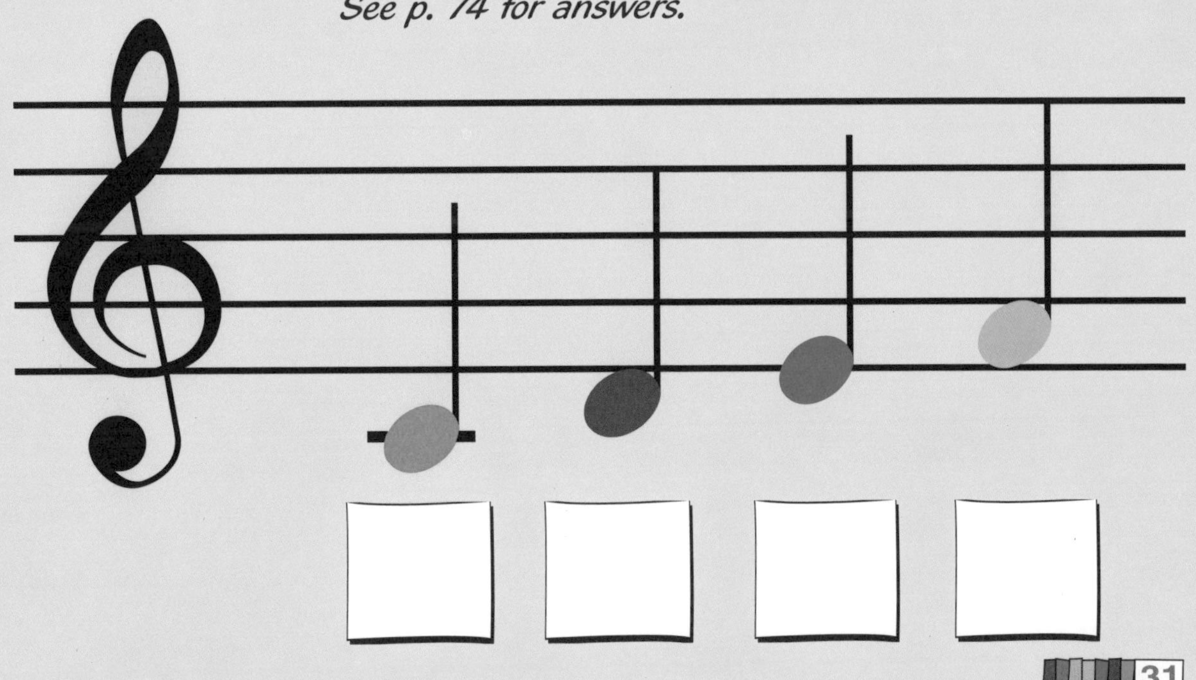

# Pet's Concert

Count: 1 2 3 4 1 2 3 4

"Wow, wow" barks the dog - gy,

1 2 3 4 1 2 3 4

"Meow, meow" goes the Kit - ty cat.

MORG

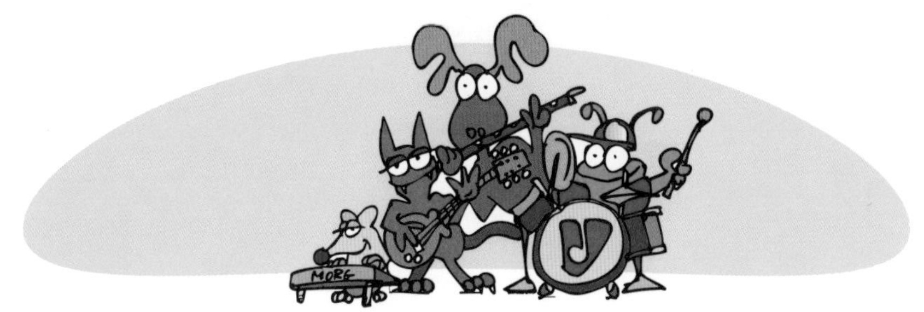

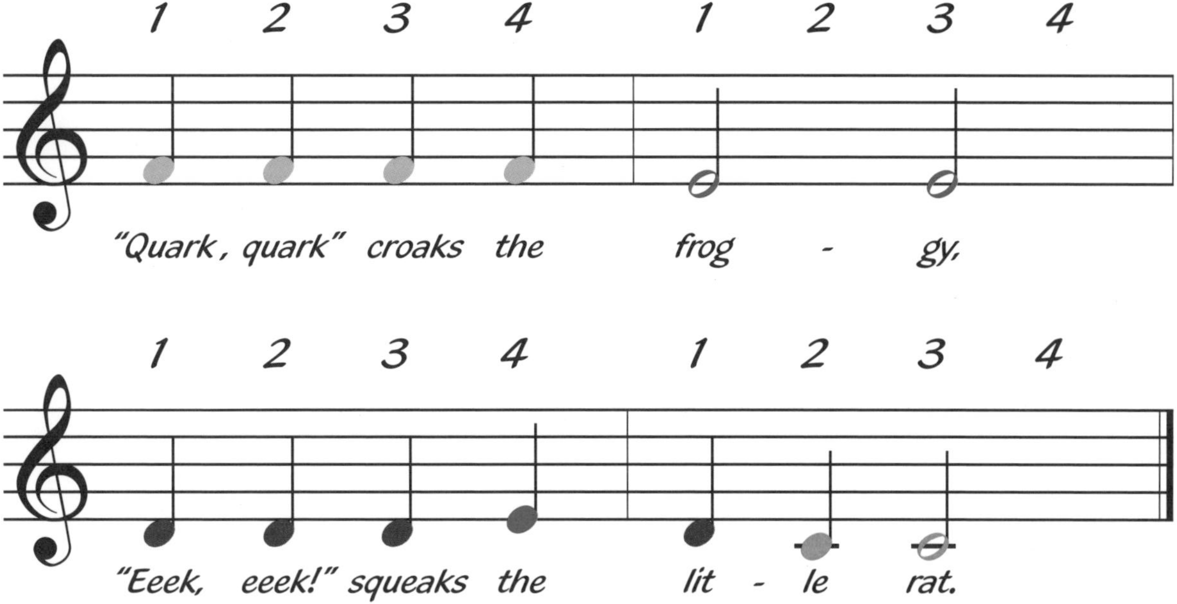
1 2 3 4 1 2 3 4
"Quark, quark" croaks the frog - gy,
1 2 3 4 1 2 3 4
"Eeek, eeek!" squeaks the lit - le rat.

# Home Again

Count: 1 2 3 4 1 2 3 4

Lit - tle train, move a - gain,

1 2 3 4 1 2 3 4

take me down the rail - way.

1 2 3 4 1 2 3 4
Stop a - gain, lit - tle train,
1 2 3 4 1 2 3 4
and I will be home a - gain.

# The Note G

*Once you have learned the note G you will know more than half of the notes on your glockenspiel. The note that represents the tone G is located on the second line from the bottom of the staff. It has a grey note head.*

***The Note G***

*Here are all the notes that you know already. Try playing them on your glockenspiel – in a nice, even tone.*

# Once a Man

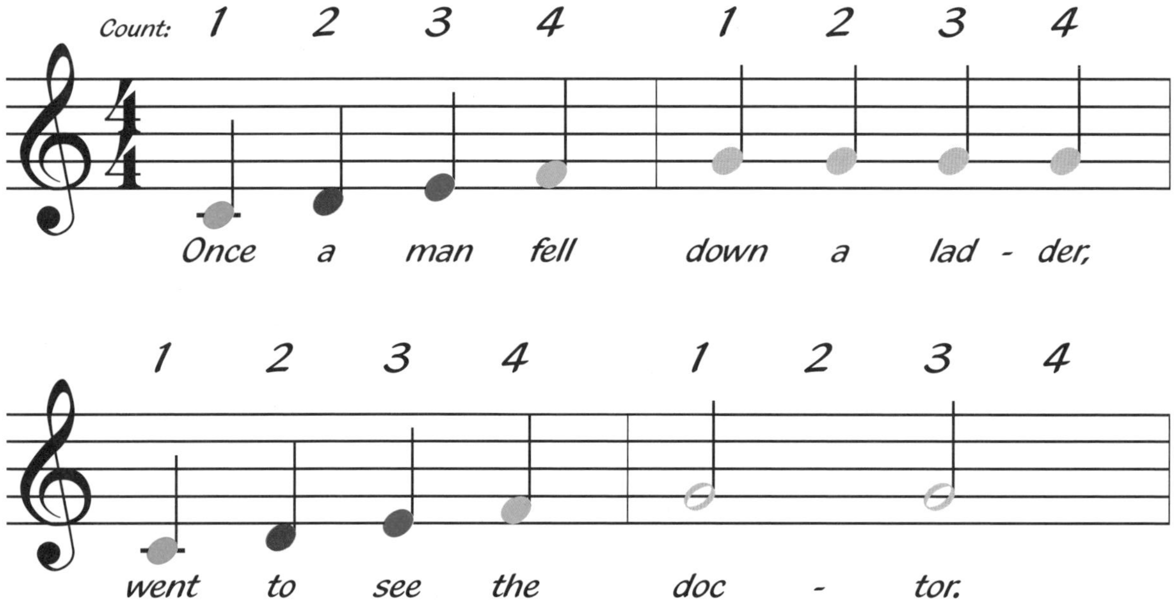

Count: 1 2 3 4 1 2 3 4

Once a man fell down a lad - der,

1 2 3 4 1 2 3 4

went to see the doc - tor.

1 2 3 4 1 2 3 4

If he had - n't fal - len down, he

1 2 3 4 1 2 3 4

would - n't need a doc - tor.

# Whole Notes (Semibreves)

*You are already familiar with the* ***quarter note*** *and the* ***half note.*** *Take a look at the following illustration as a reminder of how to count these notes best.*

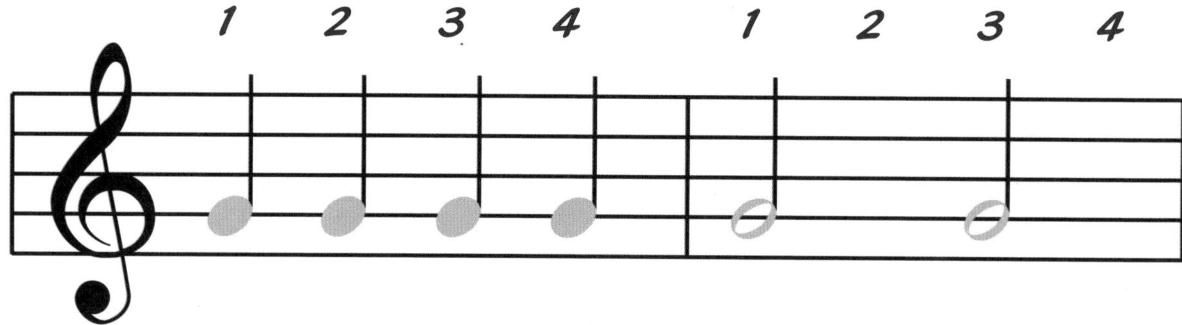


*But there is a note that is even longer than the half note – we call it a* ***whole note*** *or semibreve.*

*Whole note*

*This is what the* ***whole note*** *looks like.*
*It has an unfilled note head, just like the half note. But if you look really closely you will see that the note head looks a little different to that of the half note. But the most important aspect is that the whole note has no note stem.*

*The whole note lasts for four beats. So you strike the bar of your glockenspiel and allow it to sound until you have finished counting from one to four. Here you see all the notes again:*

# Little Jack

*This tune is quite long and difficult ...*

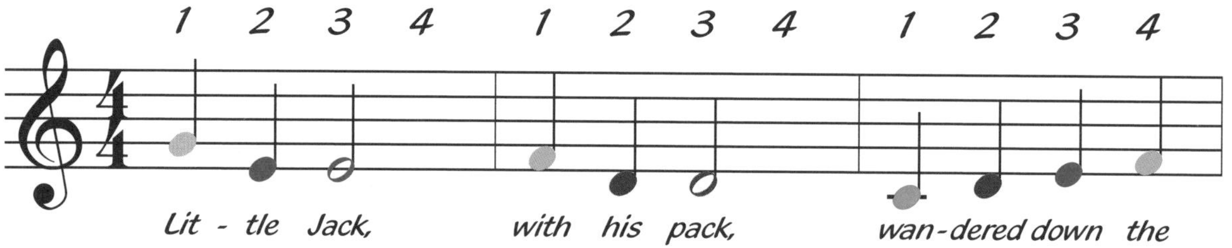


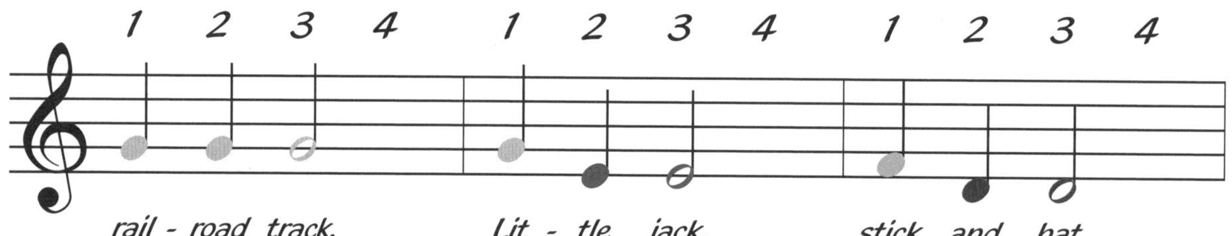

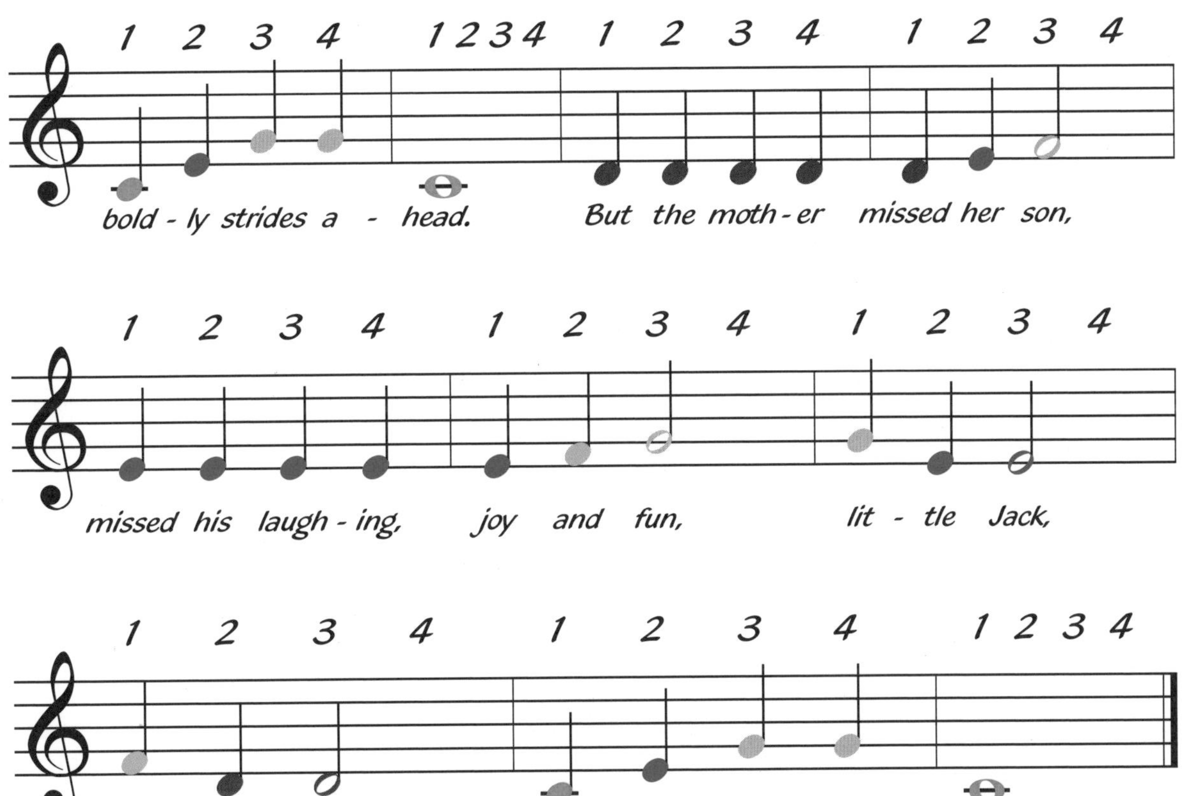
1 2 3 4 1 2 3 4 1 2 3 4 1 2 3 4
bold - ly strides a - head. But the moth - er missed her son,
1 2 3 4 1 2 3 4 1 2 3 4
missed his laugh - ing, joy and fun, lit - tle Jack,
1 2 3 4 1 2 3 4 1 2 3 4
thought a - gain, home a - gain he came.

# Merrily We Roll Along

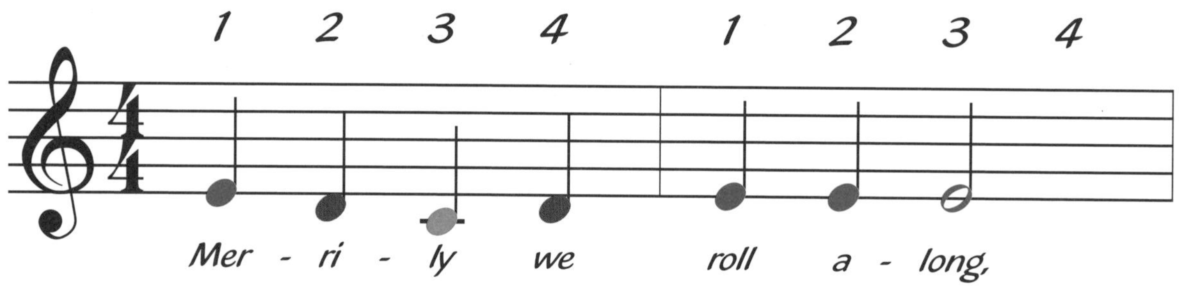


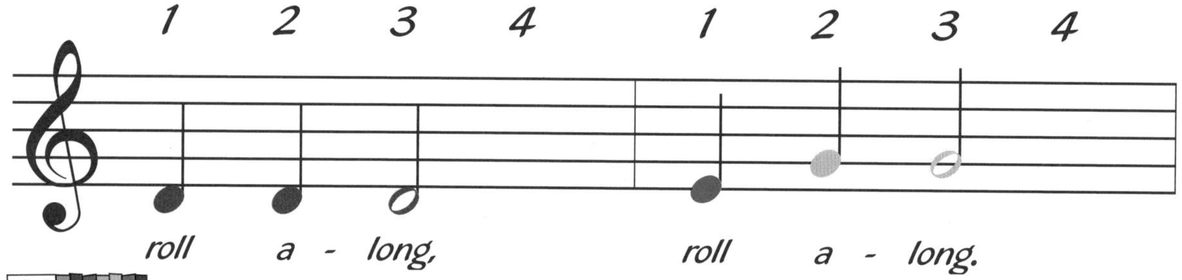

NOGGY

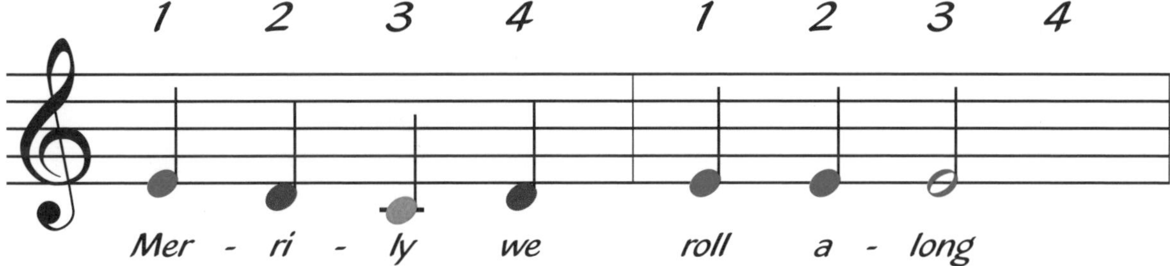
1 2 3 4 1 2 3 4
Mer - ri - ly we roll a - long

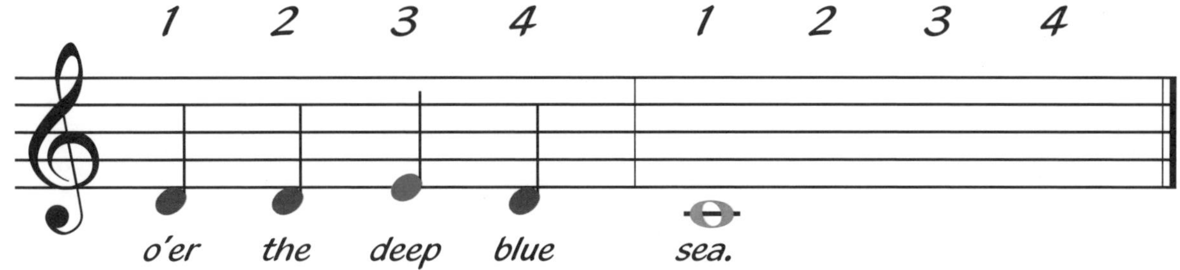
1 2 3 4 1 2 3 4
o'er the deep blue sea.

# The Note A

*Blue is our next color.
It stands for the note A.
You will find it located
two spaces up from the
bottom line.*

*The note A*

# Color this picture!

# London Bridge Is Falling Down

1 2 3 4 1 2 3 4

Lon - don Bridge is fall - ing down,

1 2 3 4 1 2 3 4

fall - ing down, fall - ing down,

VOGGY

1 2 3 4 1 2 3 4
Lon - don Bridge is fall - ing down

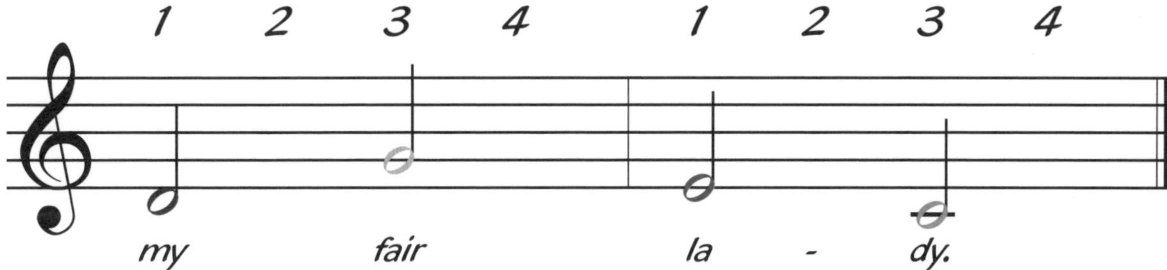
1 2 3 4 1 2 3 4
my fair la - dy.

# All My Ducks

13
Count: 1 2 3 4 1 2 3 4
All my ducks are swim - ming,
1 2 3 4 1 2 3 4
swim - ming 'round and 'round,

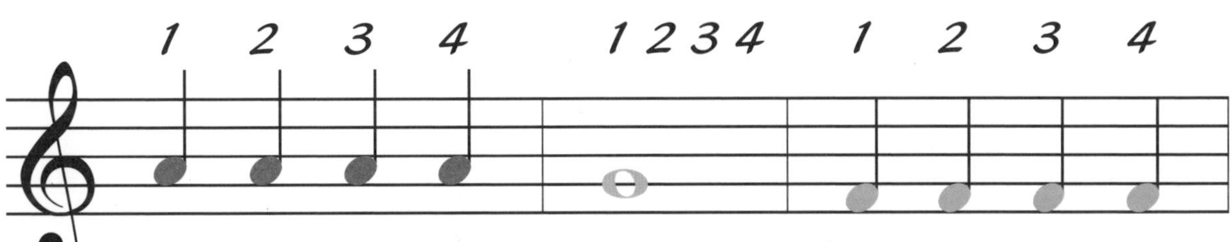
1 2 3 4
1 2 3 4
1 2 3 4
swim-ming 'round and 'round. With their tails in

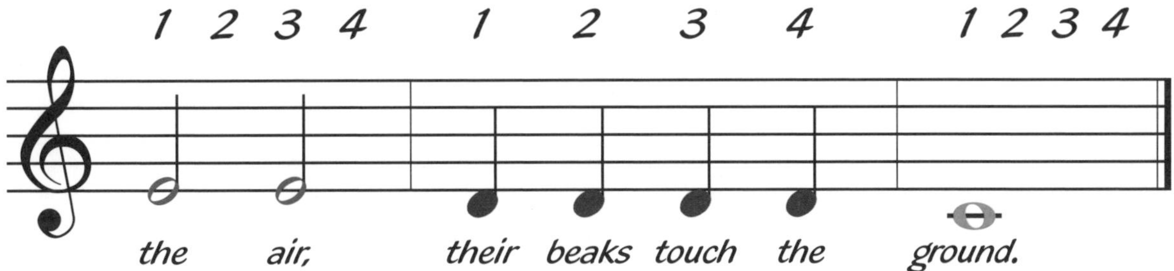
1 2 3 4
1 2 3 4
1 2 3 4
the air, their beaks touch the ground.

# Test

*Do you still remember what these are called?*

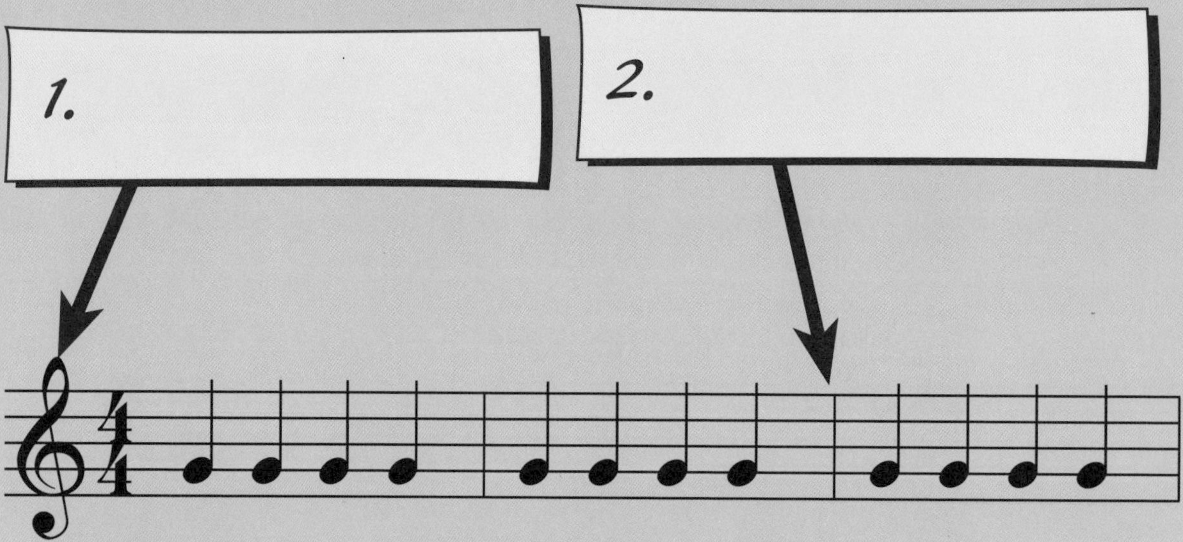

1.

2.

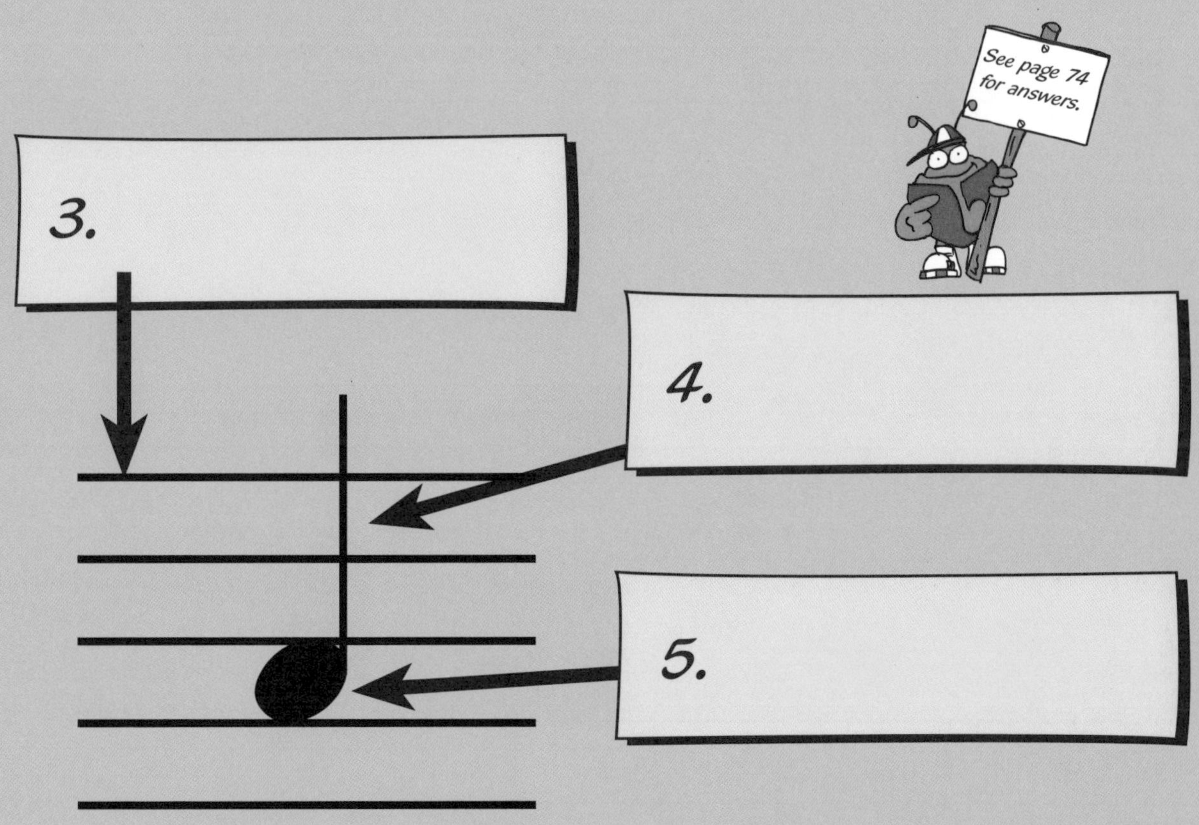


See page 74 for answers.

# The Squirrel

14

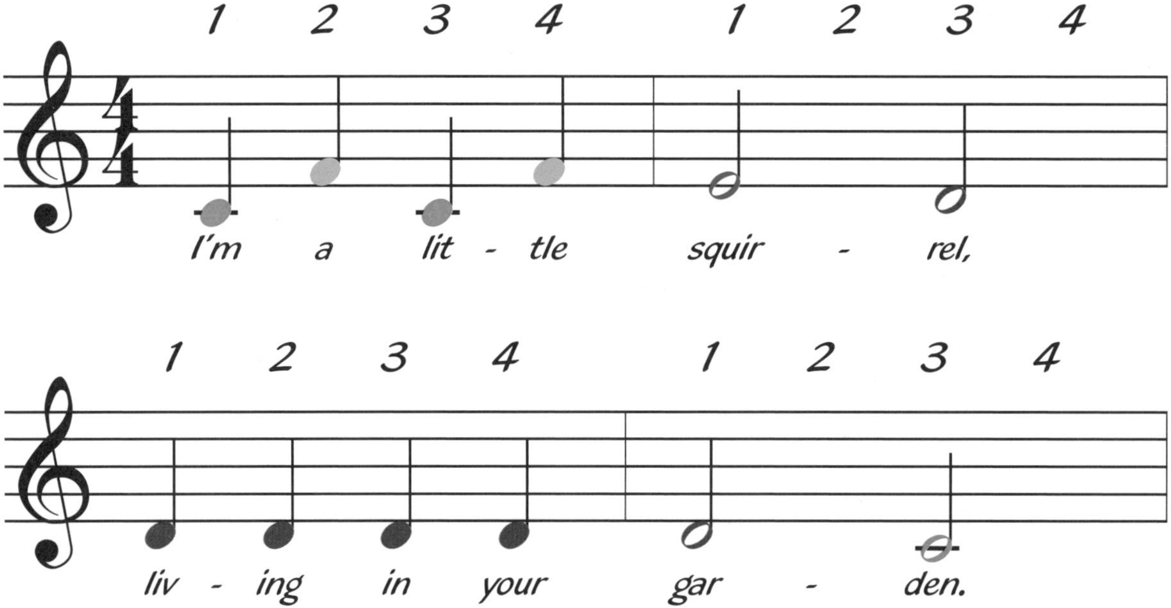
1 2 3 4 1 2 3 4
I'm a lit - tle squir - rel,
1 2 3 4 1 2 3 4
liv - ing in your gar - den.

1 2 3 4 1 2 3 4
Up and down the trees I go,
1 2 3 4 1 2 3 4 1 2 3 4
nuts and ber - ries I like so. I'm a lit - tle
1 2 3 4 1 2 3 4 1 2 3 4
squir - rel, here I go.

# Ringo, Ringo, Rango

15

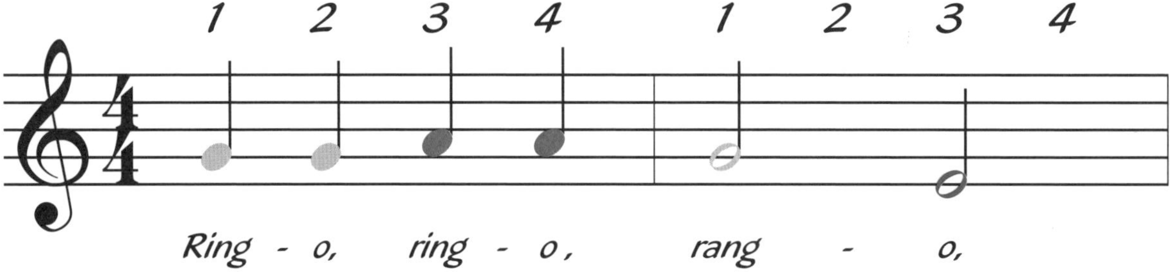
1 2 3 4 1 2 3 4
Ring - o, ring - o, rang - o,

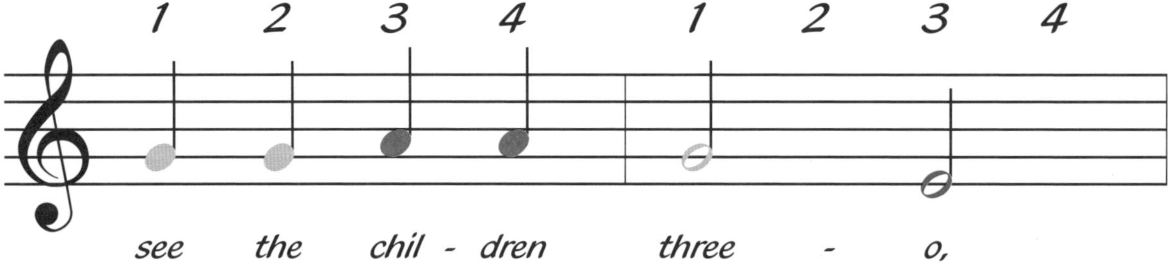
1 2 3 4 1 2 3 4
see the chil - dren three - o,

1 2 3 4 1 2 3 4
sit - ting by the li - lac bush,
1 2 3 4 1 2 3 4
all to - geth - er hush, hush, hush.

# Bunny in the Meadow

*Attention: This tune should be played fast!*

1 2 3 4 1 2 3 4

*Bun - ny in the mea - dow,*

1 2 3 4 1 2 3 4 1 2 3 4 1 2 3 4

*sits and weeps, sits and weeps.*

1 2 3 4 1 2 3 4
Lit - tle bun - ny feel - ing ill,
1 2 3 4 1 2 3 4 1 2 3 4
send the doc - tor, take a pill. Take a pill
1 2 3 4 1 2 3 4 1 2 3 4
and get well, bun - ny mine.

# Twinkle, Twinkle, Little Star

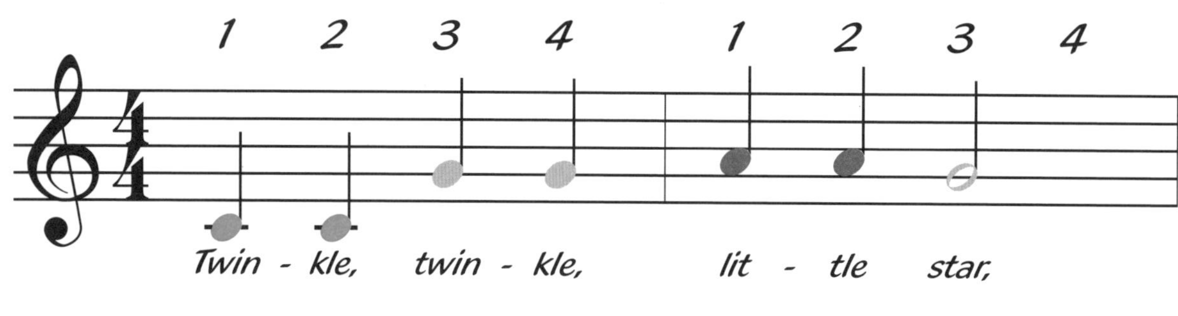

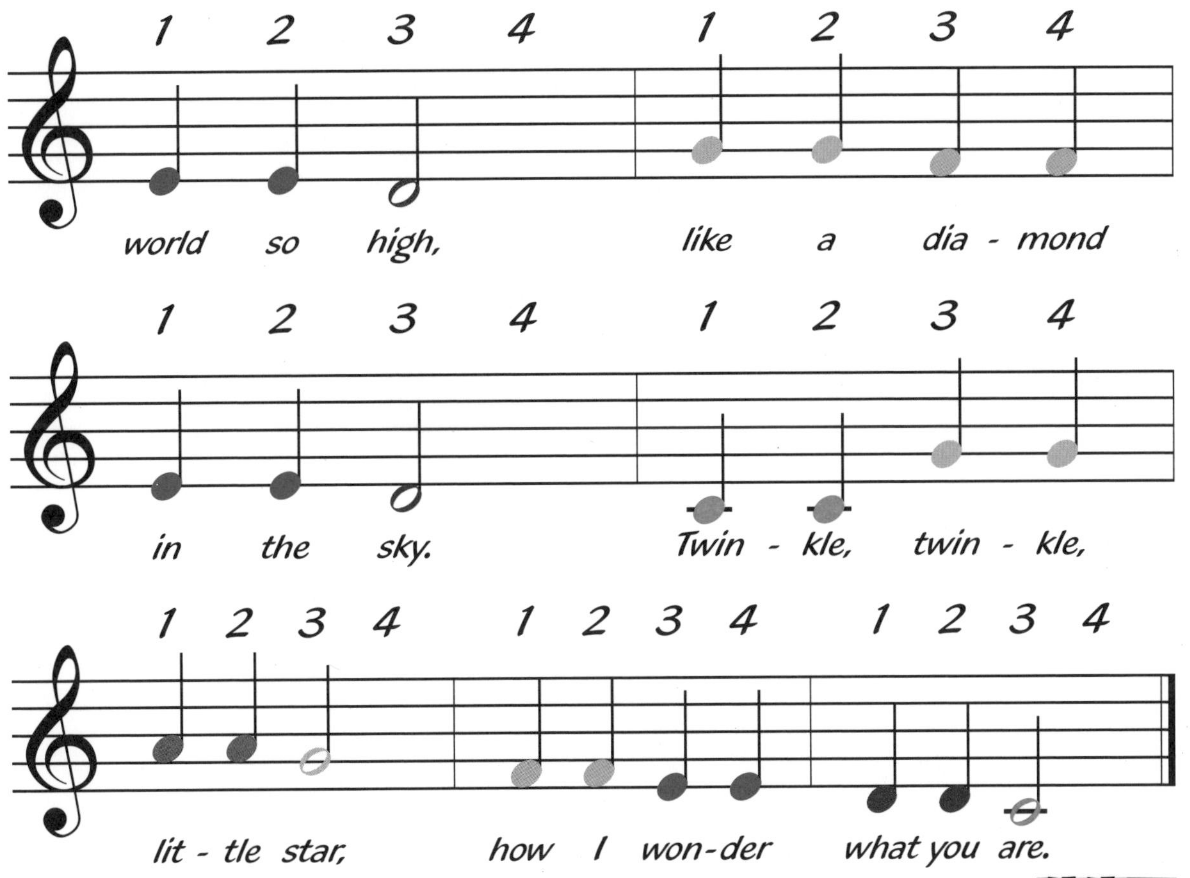
1 2 3 4 1 2 3 4
world so high, like a dia - mond
1 2 3 4 1 2 3 4
in the sky. Twin - kle, twin - kle,
1 2 3 4 1 2 3 4 1 2 3 4
lit - tle star, how I won-der what you are.

# *The Note B*

*This is the last note but one on your glockenspiel.*

*The* ***note B*** *can be found on the second bar from the right, or in other words on the second-smallest bar. The color of this note is* ***purple.***

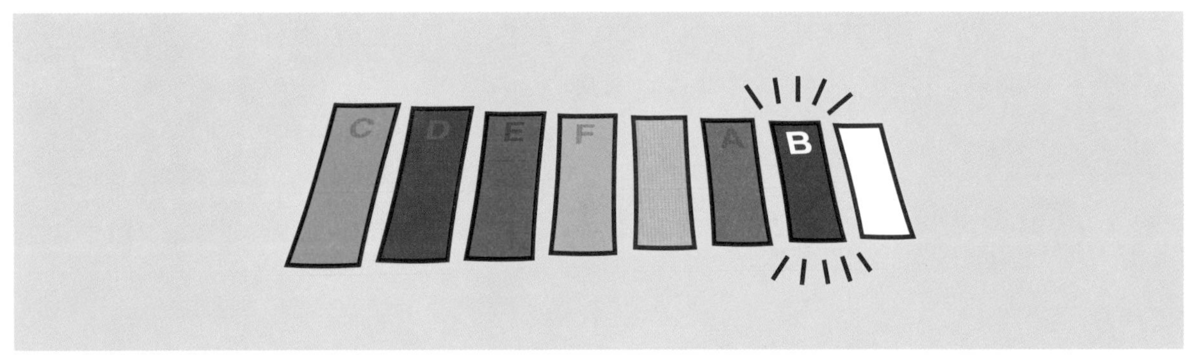

*This note looks different because the note stem points downwards.*

***Follow this simple rule:***

*If the head of the note lies on or above the middle line of the staff, the note stem points downwards.*

***The note B***

# Sleep Tight

18

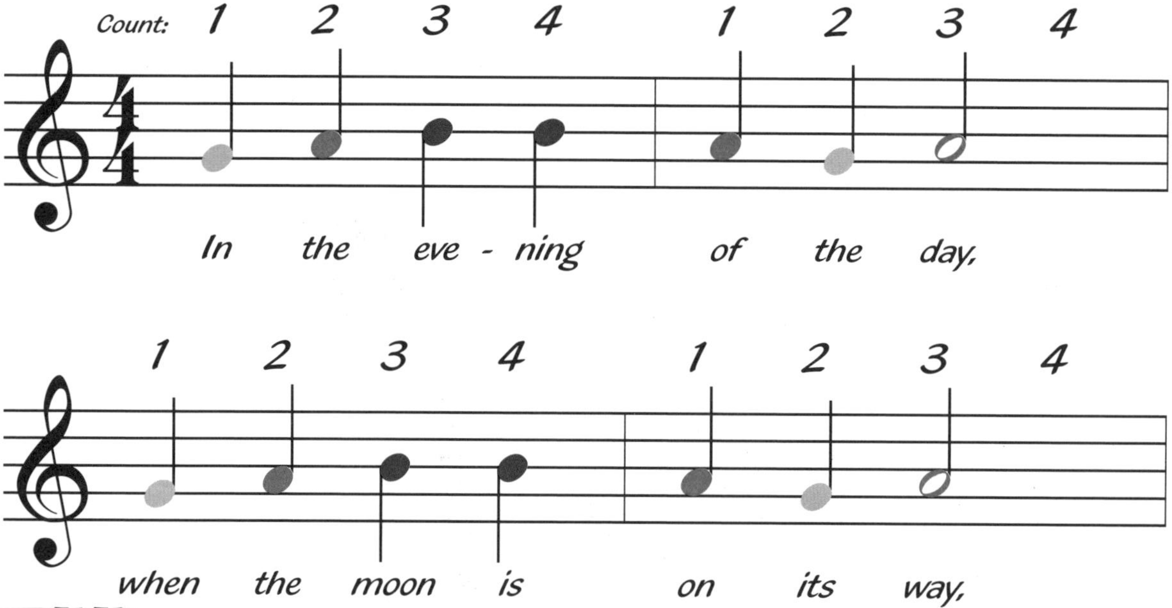
Count: 1 2 3 4 1 2 3 4
In the eve - ning of the day,
1 2 3 4 1 2 3 4
when the moon is on its way,

1 2 3 4 1 2 3 4

just sleep tight, just sleep tight,

1 2 3 4 1 2 3 4

just sleep tight my ba - by child.

# High C

*We have already learned the note C. It's found on the bar located at the far left of your glockenspiel.*

*But there's also another note called C. You will find it on the bar furthest to your right. It is twice as high as the other tone, which is why we call it "high C". We'll use the color green.*

*Just like with B, the note stem on high C points downwards.*

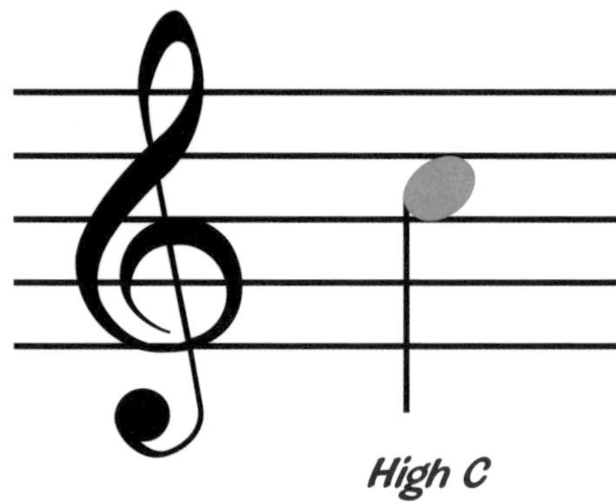

High C

*C and high C shown next to each other*

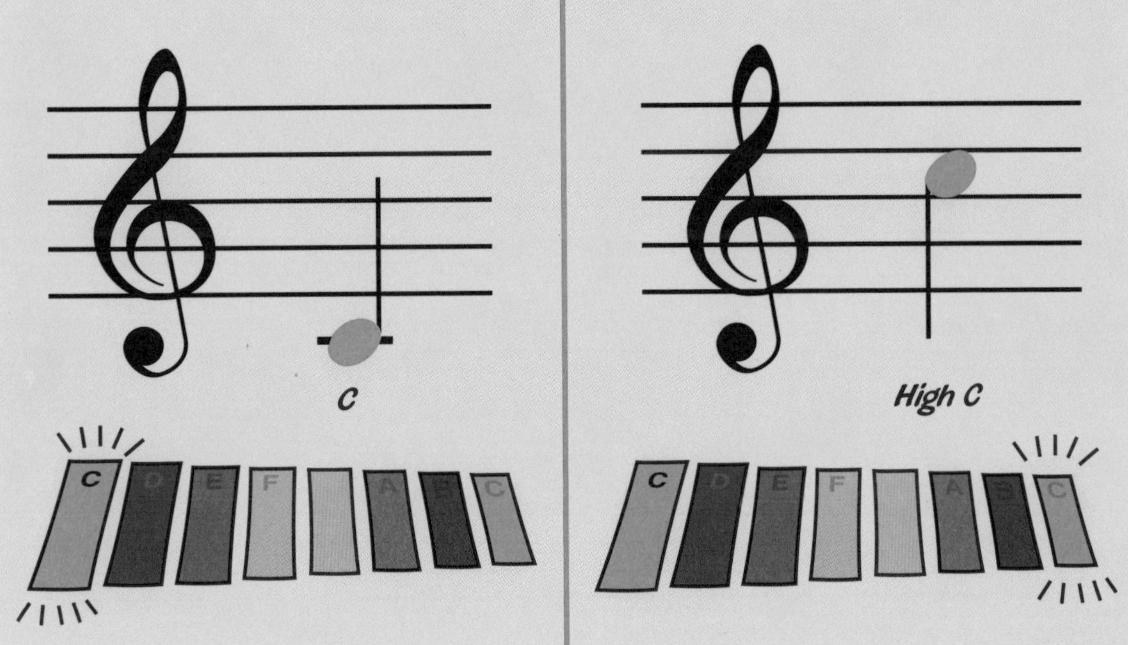

# Little Pussy

19

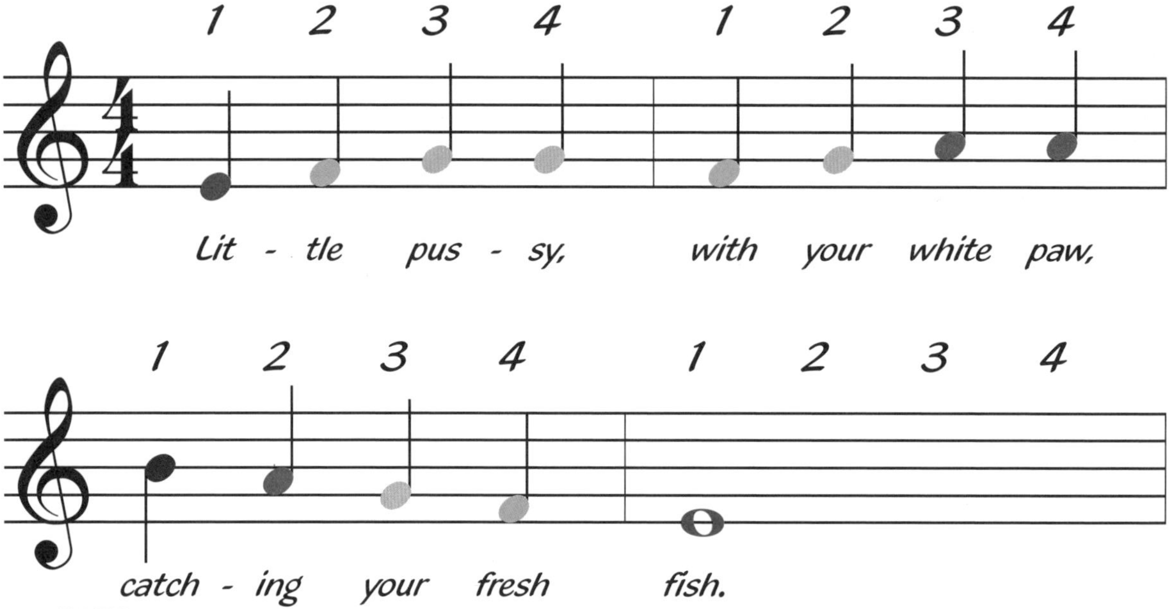
1 2 3 4 1 2 3 4
Lit - tle pus - sy, with your white paw,
1 2 3 4 1 2 3 4
catch - ing your fresh fish.

1 2 3 4 1 2 3 4
In your dain - ty pus - sy way, you'll
1 2 3 4 1 2 3 4
hide them in your niche.

# Little Fox

1 2 3 4 1 2 3 4

Lit - le fox, you stole my gos - ling,

1 2 3 4 1 2 3 4 1 2 3 4

give it back a - gain, give it back a -

1 2 3 4 1 2 3 4 1 2 3 4
gain. If you keep my lit - tle gos - ling,
1 2 3 4 1 2 3 4 1 2 3 4
I will send a hun - ter man. He will hunt you,
1 2 3 4 1 2 3 4 1 2 3 4
he will hunt you, get you in the end.

# Big Note Test

*Here are all the notes that you have learned once more. Write the names in the boxes. When you have written down all the names correctly, you can award yourself the certificate shown on the next page.*

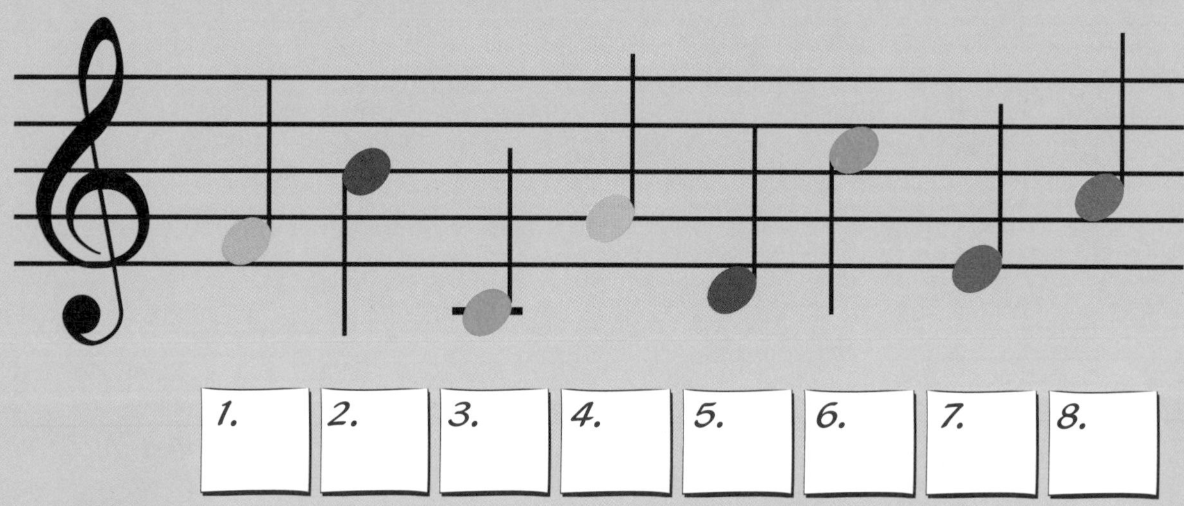

# Certificate

.................................

*has successfully learned the notes*
*C, D, E, F, G, A, B and high C.*

# Answers

*Here are the answers to my little quizzes and test*

*Page 31* *C, D, E, F*

*Page 52/53*

1. *Clef*
2. *Bar line*
3. *Staff line*
4. *Note stem*
5. *Note head*

*Page 72* *F, B, C, G, D, (high) C, E, A*

# The Note Cake

*Imagine a measure as being like a cake.*

*A **whole note** is like a whole cake.*

*Two **half notes** are like a cake cut into two halves.*

*Four **quarter notes** are like a cake cut into four quarters.*

# The Notes on Your Glockenspiel

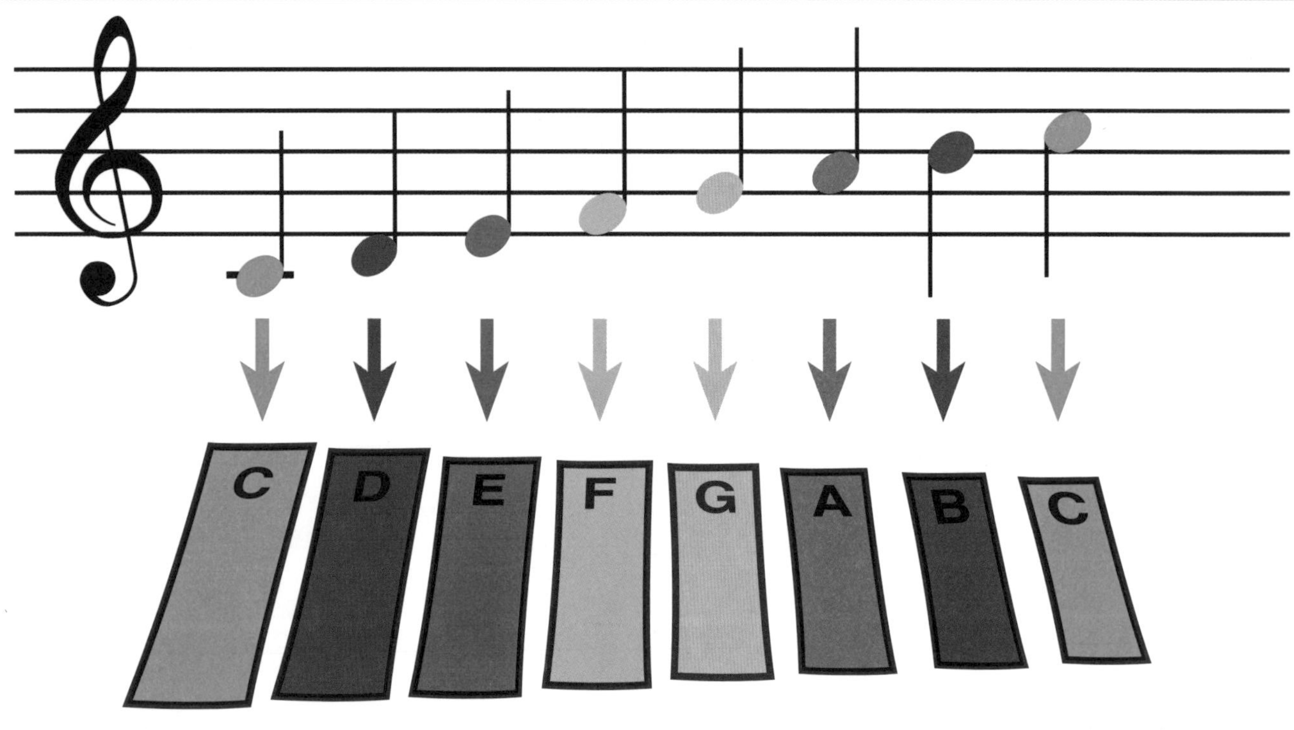

# Alphabetical List of Tunes

# *Using the CD*

*All the tunes showing me with a CD in my hand can be found on the CD.*
*I'll hold up a sign to let you know which number.*
*To make playing along easy, I've recorded every song in three versions, directly following each other:*

1. *The whole song. This version is for you to listen to and get a general idea of how it's supposed to sound.*
2. *In this version the melody is much softer. You can use it as a "guide" to help you play along.*
3. *This version only features the accompaniment. Here it's up to you alone to play the melody.*

# CD Titles

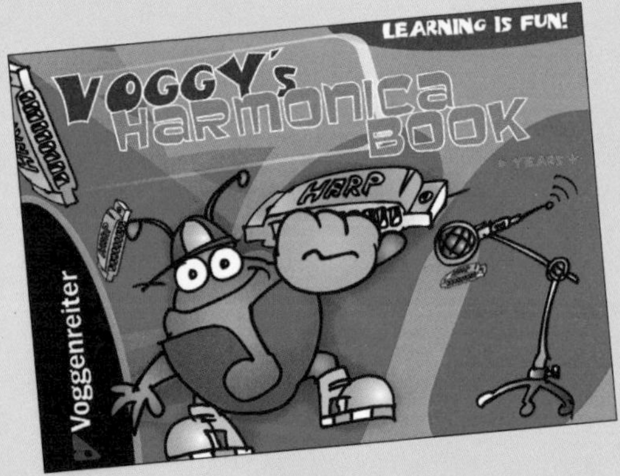


## Voggy's Harmonica Book

Little Voggy accompanies your child on the harmonica on his adventure and discovery tours through the fascinating world of music. From the correct way to hold and play it, to learning individual notes, reading music and playing whole tunes. Everything is comprehensively explained in simple terms. For diatonic and Richter harmonicas (Blues harp) in C.

DIN A5 landscape format,
ring binding, 96 pages,
with accompanying CD
ISBN 3-8024-0461-0

## VOGGY's Recorder Book

No other instrument compares with the recorder for early musical contact. Accompanied by little Voggy, your child will discover this fascinating world, step by step. From the correct way to hold and play the recorder, to learning individual notes, reading music and playing whole tunes. Everything is comprehensively explained in simple terms.

DIN A5 landscape format,
ring binding, 112 pages
ISBN 3-8024-0464-5